THE WOLF
WOMAN

BY

H. BEDFORD-JONES

British Library Cataloguing-in-Publication Data
A catalogue record for this book is available from the
British Library

CONTENTS

H. BEDFORD-JONES

Henry James O'Brien Bedford-Jones was born in Napanee, Ontario, Canada in 1887. He was raised in the western Canadian provinces and moved to Michigan after a year of college. Here, as a reporter for a local newspaper, he became a close friend of well-known pulp writer William Wallace Cook. It was Cook who helped Bedford-Jones break into pulp magazines in 1909.

From 1910 to 1913, Bedford-Jones lived in Chicago. Here, he worked in a variety of jobs, from secretary to railroad magnate to newspaper stringer, while tirelessly churning out quite literally millions of words for the pulp magazines. Between 1914 and 1923, he wrote in excess of 3 million words for *People's* magazine alone, in addition to publishing work in a variety of other magazines, such as *Argosy, All-Story, Blue Book* and *Top-Notch*, under both his own name and a range of pseudonyms. By 1914, he had moved permanently to the Los Angeles area, though his restlessness led him to live temporarily in a variety of places over the next two decades. During this time, Bedford-Jones achieved the distinction of becoming the most prolific contributor to *Blue Book*, with a total of around 350 short stories and novelettes, and thirteen serialized novels. Some of his best-known short stories published in *Blue Book* include 'Arms and Men', 'Ships and Men', 'Flags of Our

Fathers' and 'Warriors in Exile'.

Perhaps fittingly for an author who cited Alexandre Dumas as his chief influence, Bedford-Jones' adventure stories were set in both historical and contemporary times, in many locales and exotic areas across the globe. However, despite producing eighty books and nearly 1,400 magazine novels, serials and short stories, and earning the nickname 'King of the Pulps' during his life, Bedford-Jones is relatively unheard-of today. His death from heart failure marked the effective end of the pulp era.

THE WOLF WOMAN

H. Bedford-Jones

(*The Blue Book*)

Norman Fletcher phoned me one morning. Even though one may know Fletcher well, to get a call from so distinguished a scientist—one of the great men of the earth—is to get a thrill.

"Hello!" came his cheerful tones. "Have you a stenographer in your office?"

"Yes," I replied in some astonishment.

He chuckled. "Have you a particular young woman there named Stephens?"

"Oh! Sure. Why?"

"I have a letter from her."

"You have what?"

"I got a letter from her the other day, asking if I could reveal the origin of the werewolf myth. If you're not busy, will you bring her out this evening?"

"Of course!" I promised. "I've been meaning to get in touch with you. The Inventors' Club want to know whether you'll be good enough to give any more demonstrations—"

"No!" he barked, with an unwonted brusqueness. "Sorry; I've undertaken a lot of Government work and may leave for Washington soon. Besides, something's gone wrong with my apparatus. Apparently it's getting out of control; I'll explain tonight."

I hung up, thinking uneasily of the recent occasion when something had gone wrong with his infernal invention. Then I called Miss Stephens and she flushed when I told her of Fletcher's words.

"Perhaps it was terribly impertinent," she confessed. "But you had said so much about those experiments—and I did a thesis at college on the werewolf—and, well—"

"And all that remains is for you to drive out there with me tonight," I said cheerfully. "You'll have the last word—or the first word—on the werewolf subject."

She was demure enough as I ushered her into Norman Fletcher's laboratory that evening and performed the introductions; but her demure quality had solid sub-surface foundations. In no time at all, she had Fletcher interested, for she knew her subject; everything that had been written about werewolves, or humans who took wolf form at night, was in her head.

"But where's your apparatus?" she exclaimed, looking around. "Working with ultrasonic and high-frequency waves, with electricity of all sorts—and nothing in sight!"

It is true that about this grim stonewalled laboratory was little to suggest the home of the most advanced electrical scientist in the country. Easy-chairs were grouped about his instrument-board, or controls; this, looking like the triple manual of an organ, gave forth a faint hum of tubes at heat, but seemed unconnected with any other apparatus.

Fletcher settled himself before it and dimmed the room lights. To my displeasure, Miss Stephens accepted a cigarette and smoked with an air of enjoyment. She knows very well that I discourage cigarettes about the office, but she disregarded me entirely and seemed absorbed in Fletcher and his theories.

"Reduced to its essentials," Fletcher said, "the myth is that a person dons a girdle of wolf-skin and turns into a wolf, to prowl at night; a woman is usually the subject, and as a rule it makes a grisly and horrible story. It goes back to the earliest of the Greek writers, even back to the Assyrians, and the belief still lingers in Europe today."

"Yes," said Miss Stephens. "I have Vetlugin's book on the Russian legends about it."

"Oddly enough," pursued old Fletcher, "the werewolves of the Christian dispensation were usually beneficent creatures, even touching and pitiful. While attempting yesterday to discover the origin of the legend, I chanced upon the story I'm going to show you. It concerns St Odo, abbot of Cluny."

That his singular genius actually brought back scenes and sounds of the past, that the tremendous power of his ultrasonic mechanism could recapture, by a sort of backward television, real incidents from across the ages, we already knew. There was much about his process, however, that he had never revealed to anyone.

"Then," I said, "the characters tonight will talk old French, I presume?"

"No," said Fletcher hurriedly, for already the yellowish light was beginning to play upon the stone wall facing us. "My apparatus is somehow out of kilter; it does unexpected things, I regret to say, and I've no time to work on it now. Something about those new tubes and the iridium I've been using."

"What's that got to do with the language employed?" I asked.

"Everything. I can now get the sound alone, or the scenes alone. Yesterday I made a recording of the sound on this story and rushed it up to the university. Professor Hartmetz translated it into English and had the words recorded anew, rushed it back to me by dinnertime tonight, and I now switch the recording in on my sound-track. Ah! Pardon me."

A telephone was buzzing insistently. He reached out to the instrument and spoke. I watched the yellowish light dissolving the stones of the wall; the solid granite melted and began to disappear before our eyes. Suddenly Fletcher's voice sounded sharply.

"What?" he ejaculated. "What's that, Hartmetz? A horrible thing? Impossible! It was a lovely story, about St Odo and the wolves—what? It was not?" Agitation suddenly thrilled in his tones. "Good Lord, man! Then there must be something wrong! Well, let it go. Thanks for calling me. I've got the thing on now. Good night."

I vaguely realised that something in his programme had gone decidedly amiss; in the reflected radiance I saw him mop his brow and dart an anxious look at Miss Stephens, but she did not notice. She was staring at the wall. Those solid stones had now almost vanished, and as through a window, we were gazing out upon a scene that was no picture, but reality in every dimension. I caught a dazed mutter from Norman Fletcher.

"Sanscrit, he says—Sanscrit! The old Aryan race, thousands of years ago; no, no, it's impossible. . . ."

A woman's laughter drowned out the mutter.

The scene before us blurred and moved, blurred and took

shape anew—a vista of hills and forests, of squat, massive towers. Again everything blurred; the apparatus was certainly not functioning aright. The woman's laughter rose louder; it was no ringing musical peal of mirth, but the bitter laughter of hysteria. Suddenly the scene came clearly.

She was standing in a courtyard, laughing; a glorious figure against the background of rough stone and ancient thick trees, a woman laughing wildly, torn between grief and furious anger. The group of men regarded her with fear and awe. Her laughter died out and she put both hands to her face, as though to shut out some frightful vision.

This whole scene conveyed an impression of indescribable savage majesty; one sensed it, felt it in every detail. In this place was no delicacy or grace. The courtyard, the walls and buildings, were of enormous ill-fitted stone blocks; the trees were nobly massive; an air of spacious power pervaded everything, as in some dwelling of the gods.

The very doors, the stone seat, the beam-ends under the eaves, were gigantic and heavy-hewed. The weapons of the men bulked crudely large; spears with great bronze blades, huge splay-bladed axes of bronze, swords like beams of metal. The men themselves were built to match—figures of muscled strength and power. Out-stretched at the woman's feet, red tongue lolling was a tamed wolf of tremendous size, eyeing her sharply.

The woman lifted her head and bared her face. She was in

white, a golden torque about her neck. Her radiant loveliness struck forth like sun through dark clouds; it was a regal beauty, a richly glowing force instinct with energy. There was nothing passive about her. Into her stark blue eyes came a flame that shook her whole body, and her voice leaped forth like a clarion.

"Fight, Shatra! I'll lead, with you and the warriors following."

"Very well, but you know what it means, Indra," said the stalwart warrior, Shatra. "You know how they kill us; all day long we slay the little dark men, and at the end when we're exhausted, they overwhelm us. They're in countless numbers like ants. That's how your husband the king died; that's how most of our warriors have died. We are few, and they are like the forest leaves. Barbarians, rude and uncouth and swart—but they fight!

"That," he went on sadly, "is how our Aryan people have vanished. They slew in vain, and were overwhelmed. They drifted away and migrated, their civilisation is lost; these little dark men have swarmed over the whole land. We alone remain, and now it is our time to die, if so you command."

The flame died from Indra's face.

"You have sworn to obey me and my son to the death," she said quietly.

"Our oaths stand; order it, and we fight and die—you and

your son with us."

She caught her breath. "I see, I see! What are their terms?"

"They will not attack; behind our walls we can stand and laugh at them, killing them as they come. Their king gives a choice. Go forth freely and migrate, unharmed, seek another land as most of our people have done. Or else remain here in our stronghold; they'll send us what we need of food, but every man of us who leaves the walls, will be slain; women and children taken for slaves. We are the last of our people, Indra; the choice is yours to make and we abide by it."

She listened, wide-eyed. "Clever, these people! Let us remain here—and any who go forth, die! They're not anxious for any fight to the death. Come."

She beckoned imperiously and started across the courtyard. They followed her, mounting by the stairs to the stone tower over the gateway.

This was the donjon or central keep, the palace quarters of the dead king of a vanished people. From the squat tower, Indra could look down into the courtyard of the crudely massive castle itself, whose walls stretched afar over the hill. Within these walls was a small town. Outside was a vast camp stretching afar by hill and forest. And, from this camp, a score of the besiegers had come into the great courtyard of the castle, and waited there.

Indra looked at them. Hardy, swarthy men, different from her own people; smaller in stature, armed only with sword and bow. No stalwart hunters, like her powerful race, but numberless as the sea sands in that vast camp, an ocean of men who had flooded down over the snowy peaks and had driven her people out of their land. Small men, these Dravidians, yet they had conquered the mighty Aryan people and driven them into migration and exile afar.

"Perhaps it were better to go, like the rest," she murmured.

"We could take nothing, Indra," said one of her chiefs. "We must leave all arms and all treasure."

Her lips firmed. Her eyes flashed.

"No, then!" she exclaimed. "No! Keep our arms and our city; we, the last of our race!"

The chieftains assented and went to tell the Dravidian envoys. Indra, looking out upon the hills, perceived the deep cunning of these small people.

On the hills and slopes all about the town and castle, were palaces and chateaux. The Aryan princes and nobles had used these, for coolness in summer, for hunting in the winter; now the Dravidians occupied them, and the owners were dead. She perceived that the swarthy warriors thus held the place in a cordon. Their main host could go its ways and they would wait, grimly.

The summer had ended, autumn was whistling over the mountains, the first snow would fall any day now. Indra lifted unseeing eyes to the southward. There, over the vast lands that stretched to the sea and the ends of earth, the dark people had moved in. The Aryans had gone, scattered in migration after migration to the west and north, over the horizon to destiny unknown. Here among the mountains were the final remnant.

Her husband had fallen, the princes and great men had fallen. They had slain until they were borne down by sheer weight of numbers, like a man defying the tide to cover him. She, and the last of her people, and the boy who should some day be a king—her son; these were left. A king? Over what? There was no longer a kingdom. There would be no more a people over which he could rule, when he reached manhood.

An old councillor came and pointed to the courtyard below.

"Come, Lady Indra! The king of these people comes; you must meet him before the gates and swear the oath."

"Eh? What oath?"

"To observe the treaty; that none of our people shall war against his or leave these walls. Otherwise they die. He swears to let provisions enter freely, even to supply them, and to carry no fight to us. A great oath, with all the gods to witness!"

It was so accomplished before the gates, in sight of all men, and with sacrifices to the gods. This King Savastri drew the eye of Indra. He was a man of thirty, proud of eye and bearded, very active and light on his feet despite his armour; his features held a certain humour, and men said he was merry and as a warrior unequalled. He was grave today, however, and Indra thought his dark eyes were hungry as he looked upon her.

So she swore that she would permit none of her people to make war or leave the castle. And he to his own oaths, and the people and the host bearing witness. It was published that anyone leaving the castle might be slain by the dark folk, without redress.

"Leave now, if ye like—your whole people!" said King Savastri, white teeth flashing in a laugh. "Leave, and die! The quicker it's done, the sooner we'll have your women."

His eye touched upon Indra as he spoke, but she turned away in contempt and made no reply to the taunt. Thus was the doom of the last Aryans sealed. They obeyed Indra to the letter, as they had sworn to do. Being a fierce people, they might have preferred to sally forth and die fighting, but she thought of the boy, and decided to temporise; so they obeyed, though it meant slow death for them all, cut away from the whole world.

But Indra sat in the great courtyard as the days passed, with the huge tamed wolf, Vic, at her feet; and her blue eyes flamed as reports came to her. The Dravidian host had flowed away over the hills like an ocean wave. Plenty of them remained; their leaders dwelt in the little castles and chateaux, the dark folk made villages around each one, and their king, Savastri, occupied the massive hunting-lodge built by Indra's husband, three miles away. From here, he ruled his dark people, who had taken over the whole land. The autumn rains came down, and the first touches of snow, but little frost as yet.

It was said that everywhere in the country the civilisation of the Aryan people was lost and ruined, for these Dravidians were an uncouth and ignorant race.

Indra listened to all and said little, toying now with the boy, now with the wolf. The prince was a child of four; he and the wolf were friends. A grim and fierce thing was Vic, trained to obey Indra and to defend her; the greatest of wolves, he had been captured as a pup and tamed, but his heart was savage. So large was he that the boy Shiva rode about on his back, though this did not please Vic overmuch.

On the afternoon of the first snow, with a gale sweeping over the hills and forests, Indra sent for her old councillor Ran, and for the chief warrior who remained, the stalwart Shatra. To the latter, she spoke briefly.

"Tell whatever officer commands the guard at the little postern gate in the east wall tonight, that he is to let me go out and watch for my return, without question."

"You, Indra?" exclaimed the warrior, astonished. "Who accompanies you?"

"Vic," she said. At his name, the wolf lifted head and eyed her, unwinking.

Upon Shatra fell fear and dismay.

"Lady, think twice!" he said. "In the whole country, none of our people remain except women who are enslaved. If you're found abroad and taken or killed—"

"Prince Shiva will then be in your care," she said, and dismissed him. When he had gone, she turned to the old councillor.

"Would you break the oaths you swore to the gods?" he demanded, eyeing her keenly.

"I swore much for my people; nothing for myself," she said, and this was true. "I alone can make war upon these dark folk; I alone can avenge my dead husband and our lost cities and country, our scattered people. I know secrets none other lives to know, and ways of doing this. Let's have no argument, Ran. Are they sending us cattle tomorrow?"

"It was so promised," said Ran. "A hundred head."

"Good. See to it, then, that those who bring the cattle, are told a certain story they may carry back with them: The story you used to tell me, about our ancestors who changed their shape at night and became ravening wolves."

"As ordered, I will obey," said the old man. "But what drives you to such extremes of vengeance and hatred? Why cannot you live like the rest of us—"

"Live until you die behind walls, or go forth to be killed?" she said in disdain. "If you must know, I shall bring about the death of that man who rules them."

"So?" Old Ran fingered his white beard. "Because of his look and his words, when the oath was sworn—eh? I hear he is better than his nobles and leaders; in fact, a wise ruler, a king with brains—"

Indra flushed. "A king who shall taste the vengeance of the conquered! See that the story is told them. I intend to make that man Savastri suffer before he dies. No other can kill him, but I can. The wind howling upon the thick trees howls death this night!"

"He lives in the castle your husband built, with guards and warriors—"

"And I, who helped build that castle, know its secrets," she said, smiling terribly.

Indra, who came of a warrior race, could use sword or spear better than most men.

That night, respecting her signet ring, though they could not see her face, the guards at the little east gate let her out. She was clad in a robe of wolf-skins, and the head was drawn over her head after the manner of hunters, with a flap down to conceal her face. She carried a hunting-spear, and the huge wolf Vic was at her heels. They saw her vanish into the trees where the storm tossed and the first snowflakes were drifting and sifting; and so closed the gate again, looking one at another with affrighted eyes.

Towards dawn, her voice summoned them, and the throaty

howl of Vic. A torch was brought, and recognising her, they let her in, but not as she had gone. Red was her spear, and the cruel jaws of Vic slavered blood.

"Do no talking," she ordered the guards, and went her way.

With morning, Dravidian warriors drove cattle into the great castle, as promised, and told a strange tale. Wolves had broken into the king's lodge, none knew how; one of their princes, and two of the bodyguard of the king, had been slain. The wolves had vanished again.

These men were told the legends of the royal house, and how certain of its princes could take the shape of wolves, at will. Undoubtedly, the ghost of the dead king had acted thus, taking vengeance upon his conquerors. With this cold comfort, the Dravidians were sent whence they had come.

Three days later, King Savastri and six of his chieftains came demanding speech with Indra. She had them brought up to the courtyard of the keep, and sent Vic away to the kennel he occupied; he was licking his jaws and his fur, this frosty morning.

Word spread that there had been more killing in the king's lodge, last night. Indra appeared, with Ran and others of the council behind her, and greeted the king. He saluted her, his bold eager eyes never leaving her face.

"Lady, there is peace between my people and yours, for so you have chosen," he said abruptly. "We have kept the peace;

but your people have come upon us in the night, slaying."

"That is untrue," Indra replied, and beckoned Ran. "Go and discover if any man left the gates last night or yesterday. If so, he shall die here and now for disobedience."

The old man departed, and she looked against Savastri, unsmiling and serene.

"You are no liar," he said impulsively.

"I am no liar," she rejoined. "Now tell me what has happened."

"This is the second time," he said, while his chieftains assented. "Last night two of my captains were slain—mangled as though by wolves. A guard thought he saw a wolf-shape slinking through the rooms. Evidently your people are doing this."

"If so, they shall die; I swear it," she rejoined. "Is it possible you don't know the legends of our royal house? The ghosts of the dead are visiting you, great king; the ghost of my husband, whom your warriors slew, takes a wolf-shape in the night and kills. This is the old story, for my people are hunters and forest people."

"I have heard some such story being noised abroad," said Savastri. "All nonsense! One of those captains was killed with a spear, last night. Wolves don't use spears."

"So?" She regarded him steadily, a cool smile of contempt in her eyes. "Great king, let me advise you to change your dwell-

18

ing. Seek safety elsewhere. Let your warriors occupy the royal lodge and risk the vengeance of dead men; you can hide safely in another place."

The cool mockery of her words was bitter to bear, and Savastri flushed.

"I'm not that sort, lady. By the god Shiva! I'll lay that ghost, if ghost it be!"

"Shiva?" She started slightly. "Who is he?"

"One of our gods."

"Aye? It's the name of my son—there he is, now."

The boy appeared crossing the courtyard. Savastri and his chiefs regarded him, and their stern dark faces changed and lightened with swift admiration. The boy was like a radiant sunbeam. Savastri turned quickly to Indra.

"Lady, marry me!" he said abruptly. "Marry me, and your people shall go free!"

Her eyes chilled. "When I marry you, barbarian, it will only be upon the couch of death!"

So barbed with disdain were her words that the Dravidian chieftains growled angrily, but Savastri only looked into her face and a smile leaped in his quick eyes.

"You'll be worth the having," said he. Before her fury could find response, old Ran came back and made report.

No man had left the city or passed the walls since the peace had been sworn.

"My warriors are not liars," said Indra. "Further, King

Savastri, I swear that if any man leaves the city, I'll inform you of it; if any of my people undertake any action against your people, they break my oath and their own, and shall die. Go back, and hide from the ghosts of the dead!"

There the matter ended, and she had the last word; but something in the way she said it drew a speculative, searching look from Savastri. Perhaps he suspected her from this moment.

When she heard the talk of her council and leaders, however, she went white with fury. To all of them it seemed that Savastri was the kingliest of men, and wise withal. That same night she went from the little postern gate with Vic, and returned long ere dawn; word came next day that four Dravidian chiefs, drinking together at an outpost, had been slain by a wolf—who left human tracks in the snow.

"My husband," said Indra to old Ran, "is having company on the ghost-path!"

"What good will it do you, or your people?" he asked.

Her face clouded.

"I don't know—yet. Only one thing matters to me, Ran; one person. Somehow, I shall assure his future; I shall find some way!"

"Prince Shiva was born to be a king, true," said Ran, scratching his white beard. "But the Aryan people have gone forth across the world, vanishing as a cloud in the sky; they are gone. They may found other empires afar, other races and peoples may spring from then, but they are gone. And we who remain here are doomed. Better a swineherd in safety, than a king without a kingdom or a people!"

Her blue eyes flashed. "King's blood will have king's name," said she curtly. "Three nights from now, my husband will be avenged."

Old Ran looked after her as she departed, and wagged his head sagely.

"A husband under the ground is best left there," he grumbled, "as many a woman has found to her cost ere this."

Three days passed swiftly; evening of the third day brought snow blowing through the forest trees and a keen wind whistling over the roof of the world. In this bitter night, only a beast could find his way abroad.

"Take the track, Vic," said Indra, when the gate clanged shut behind them. Obedient to her word, knowing her voice and speech, the wolf trotted ahead as she released him.

She followed close, muffled in her wolf-skins, with furred leggings, the hunting-spear in her hand. The snow now falling thicker, swirled about them, but the big wolf kept straight on, well knowing what way they went. They came at last to a thicket of trees; half a bowshot distant was the king's lodge, where a flaring cresset flickered in the storm.

Among the trees, they approached the building still more closely. Vic halted, beside a jagged rock that was rapidly piling high with snow. Indra put out her hand to it, and the mass of rock slid smoothly. Into an opening thus revealed Vic darted, but Indra called him back to heel. He obeyed, with a whine of repressed eagerness; the killer was aroused.

She passed down steps, along a tunnel, and to steps again; mounting these rapidly in the pitch blackness, she paused at a tiny gleam of light. She was now in the king's lodge, by a secret passage installed for emergencies; the others who knew of it were dead.

She touched a panel and it slid aside, letting her look into the main room, where a huge fire was dying down on the hearth. The firelight showed a number of dim figures at the door; and a voice reached her, the voice of Savastri the king.

"No, no! I remain here with two guards, and the dogs. The rest of you, out to the huts and keep watch on the grounds! I'll have no woman taunting me, even if she were the most glorious woman on earth, with skulking in safety while my captains run risks. I remain here, to meet the man-wolf if it comes. You others, stand watch outside. Go!"

They went, grumbling and protesting. One of them made some laughing remark.

"Aye," replied the king, a curiously vibrant ring in his voice. "From my first sight of that woman, my heart went out to her. I'll have no other, I tell you! There's no other in the world her equal, no other for me, and that ends it. Good night!"

Indra, listening, caught her breath in quick anger. Vic began a growl; she reached down and silenced him with a touch and a word, then looked into the room.

"The dogs are uneasy, they smell something," said a voice. She saw a guard, and two large wolfhounds, though they were somewhat smaller than Vic.

"That may be," said the king. "Both of you take the outer room, with the dogs. I'll sleep in the room beyond. Keep a light burning in your room."

An alabaster lamp was taken away, and the place was empty except for red fireglow.

Presently Indra put her weight upon the secret door, and it swung aside. About the neck of Vic was a heavy collar of wolf-skin like his own; she gripped it, and he emerged with her into the dimly lit chamber.

She did not hesitate. She was alone in the lodge with three men; two of them, and the dogs, must be killed before she could kill Savastri as she intended. She knew where lay the rooms in question; and, since she disdained to attack sleeping men, she went straight to them now—two sleeping-rooms at the end of the hall.

As she neared them, she halted, crouching. The door of the first was somewhat ajar, a light shone across the hall, a man spoke.

"I tell you, the dogs smell something—look at them! Bring the light. Let's take a turn around the place. I'll take the dogs on leash."

The dogs growled and whined; Vic's fur lifted under her hand, a savage throaty sound came from him. One of the men came out, bearing the lamp. He checked himself and put it on a stand.

"Forgot my bow," he said. "Go ahead. I'll come with the lamp."

He withdrew. The other came out, the two dogs straining on leash. They gave sudden wild tongue, sensing the presence of Vic. Indra knew it was the moment.

"Take them, Vic!" she said, and loosed him.

The great shape went hurtling for the dogs. From the guard burst a terrible cry; he frantically loosed his dogs. He had held then an instant too long. Vic was into them with the kill-growl, murderous jaws slashing too fast for eye to follow. The three shapes mingled into one—a shapeless scramble of ferocity, from which flew fur and bright drops of blood.

Indra was darting forward. The guard, long sword sweeping out, struck at the battling animals. One dog was dead, the other down. The guard sighted Indra's figure, and slashed at her as he swung around. Her spear went through him, and she tugged it free as he fell. The second dog was quivering in death and Vic was up and whirling, with fiery eyes and blood-slavering muzzle.

Out into the open came stumbling the second guard, bow bent and shaft notched. Seeing Indra, he started back. Vic went for him, and his bowstring twanged; he snatched a second shaft and shot. Both arrows thudded through the throat of the gaunt wolf, through throat to brain. The wolf's rush, however, took him at the man, leaping even as he died—leaping and slashing with cruel teeth. The guard was borne backwards, and the teeth of the dying beast ripped open his throat and chest.

"Vic! *Vic!*"

A sharp cry, as Indra darted forward. She knelt in the pool of blood. The head of the wolf lifted slightly. His eyes rolled upon her in the lamplight; then his head fell and his eyes rolled no more. He was dead. Silence, and the gusty odour of hot blood, settled upon the place.

"So men and beasts keep company down the path of ghosts!" said a voice, amused, calm, poised: the voice of King Savastri.

Indra was up, spear ready—up and flinging forward. Savastri stood in the doorway, a dagger in his left hand, a long coiled whip in his right. He wore a crimson robe and was bareheaded.

She was at him like a flash of fury. The spear drove straight for his heart, a death-blow; but it slid away from armour beneath the robe. Across her face, half masked by the flap of wolf-skin, lashed the heavy whip. Blinded, she staggered but struck again with the spear. The whip coiled about the weapon and jerked it out of her hand. The spear fell with a clatter. The

25

lash burned across her arms and body, burned again. Savastri was striking with cool, deliberate intent, but striking swiftly.

A scream burst from her. She threw herself upon him with savage ferocity. He evaded her spring, caught the wolfhead above her head, and tore it away. The fair glory of her golden hair burst forth; and the loaded whip-butt thudded down.

She crumpled without a word and lay in a huddled, inert heap.

"So!" said King Savastri, gazing at her face. "I suspected as much. Ha! Now to see where she and the beast came from."

He caught up the lamp, picked his way across the blood-spattered floor, and in the main room found the secret door ajar.

Going back quickly, he dragged the great body of Vic down the hall and to that secret door; even for his sinewy strength, it was no light task. He cut the collar from the dead wolf's neck and kept it. The beast's carcass he shoved into the hidden passage, and closed the door again.

Returning to the frightful scene of death, he picked up Indra and carried her into the farther room; she was breathing heavily, and would be unconscious a long while.

Presently King Savastri opened the door of the lodge and blew a blast on his horn. Guards came running; picking out some of the captains, he took them with him to the grisly hall, and showed them what had happened.

"The wolf came, and the wolf went," said he, showing them the collar. "You see this? Now come, and see who wore it. The stories that we heard were true."

He took them into the farther room. There upon the bed lay Indra, senseless; now she was clad in a long white robe that Savastri had put upon her, after hiding the wolfskins. He beckoned his staring captains outside and closed the door.

"Here is the girdle." He gave it to one of them. "Throw it into the fire; she will never again be able to play wolf. Rather, she remains queen!"

Indra opened her eyes to daylight and snow drifting in at the window. She lay in her own bed, in what had been her room in the royal lodge, and warm skins covered her. At her side sat King Savastri; he had been bathing her bruised head and face with a wet cloth. Now he leaned back, regarding her.

She stared at him. With a rush, memory returned; yet she was held spellbound by finding herself here and thus. She tried to speak, and could not. He smiled, leaned forward, and touched her forehead with the cloth again; his fingers were deft and very gentle.

"Apparently you had a bad dream," he said casually. "You have been talking about wolves ever since my guards found you wandering among the trees."

Her eyes dilated upon him. "Wolves?" she whispered. "Wandering? You devil! What jest is this? You know well—"

"Be quiet," broke in the king, "Be quiet and let me speak, for a little space. Here; if this will make you feel better, play with it," and he thrust a long dagger into her hand, then came to his feet and went to the window-opening.

She gripped the dagger and watched him, a flame in her eyes.

"Whatever you may think," said the king calmly, "you were picked up among the trees and brought here, by my guards. How you came here, how you left your castle, does not matter. If you're tempted to remember anything else, dear lady, it was all an evil dream. Let it be forgotten. I'm glad you're here, for I've something to say to you."

She lay like a trapped beast, wary and tense.

He came towards here, smiling. "Indra, these people of mine are a crude, savage lot of barbarians; I'm one myself. But I have sense enough to know that all the civilisation, all the fine things, of your Aryan race are perishing in the hands of my people; this whole glorious land of yours is going back to the jungle. I want to save it. You can save it. You esteem it an insult if I speak of loving you, of wedding you because you're the only woman I know who is fit to be a queen, and my wife. But there's another reason. Our people, and your son—Prince Shiva."

The name drove into her, quieted her, held her intent upon him.

"Marry me," he went on in that calm voice. "Let your people mingle with my people, let them keep all they have and more, let them teach my people your Vedic Hymns, your gods, your ways of life and art and work. The remnant of your people can grow great again, among mine; they may be a sect, a caste, apart. A superior caste, not slaves!

"I have no sons to follow me, Indra," he went on. "But with you for wife, I'd have a son, and one whom my people would worship and revere. Your boy; let me adopt him, as the future king of this people. It was not I who slew his father, but one of my captains whom your wolf killed."

"My wolf!" Her eyes widened upon him, her voice came with a catch. "Ah! Then your sorry jest is ended!"

"By the gods, I'm not jesting!" Suddenly impetuous, he came swiftly to the bed and looked down at her, and he was all ablaze. "You're no liar, Indra; you swore oaths for your people, but there was no mention of yourself in them. That gave me the clue. And what was it you said—that you would marry me only upon the couch of death? Well, you're lying upon it now; death for you and your son and your whole people, if you make that choice."

He dropped on the edge of the bed beside her, and threw out his hands.

"You have the knife; use it!" he said, hoarsely earnest. "The choice is yours. Here is my throat; kill me, if you like, if that will satisfy you! For I worship you, Indra; I worship you with my whole heart. I offer you myself, to kill or to take. . . .

"And with myself, your son's life," he went on swiftly, seeing her hand move and the knife flash. "Instead of death and ignominy, he shall have honour and a crown. Your people shall have life instead of death; this nation shall rise again—if you so choose! I offer a glorious future, worthy of you, and the name of Prince Shiva shall be enshrined among our gods. But kill me if you so desire. There is no one to interfere."

With one hand, he drew the edge of his robe over his face, and waited.

The silence of the room was stirred only by the rustle of the wintry branches outside. He could hear her quick, hard breathing, but no word came from her. Suddenly she moved and caught her breath, as though to plunge the knife into him; but he did not stir.

The knife clattered on the floor. Her hand touched his.

The scene blurred and vanished. The stone wall came back into sight, the yellow light died away, the room lights flickered on. Norman Fletcher turned to us, awe and amazement in this eyes.

"I'll be hanged!" he broke out. "This isn't what I expected to show you at all. It's not the same thing. This apparatus is playing tricks! But, my word! Did you get the meaning of what we just saw—the allusions to historic and ethnologic fact?"

"Rather!" Miss Stephens nodded, a tinge of excitement in her cheeks. "A scene from the dispersal of the great Aryan race, somewhere on the uplands of Asia, back before history began! And the legend of werewolf, which curiously enough seems to be a purely Aryan legend, a sort of race-myth!"

Fletcher stared at her.

"Well, it might have been worse," he said slowly. "I see now why Hartmetz said the language was a form of Sanscrit. And damned bloody it was, too. I'm sorry you saw it," he added apologetically.

Miss Stephens tossed her head slightly. "Why?" she rejoined coolly. "If you ask me, I thought it was fascinating, positively fascinating! All of it."

When we were driving home, I asked what she had honestly thought about it.

"Oh!" she said in her demure way, which I now realised was not really demure at all, but rather blasé, "he didn't fool me for a minute. I think he was just trying to shock me."

"Really!" I said, not without sarcasm. "And did he succeed, Miss Stephens?"

"I'm afraid," she drawled, "that poor Mr Fletcher is behind the times."

I let it go at that.

www.ingramcontent.com/pod-product-compliance
Lightning Source LLC
Chambersburg PA
CBHW030532260626
47157CB00005B/1988